THEY MAKE THE PERFECT BIRTHDAY GIFT!

BE SURE TO READ **ALL** THE **BABYMOUSE** BOOKS:

HAPPY BIRTHDAY,
BABYMOUSE

BY JENNIFER L. HOLM & MATTHEW HOLM

RANDOM HOUSE 🏠 NEW YORK

Copyright © 2014 by Jennifer Holm and Matthew Holm

All rights reserved. Published in the United States by Random House Children's Books, a division of Random House LLC, a Penguin Random House Company, New York.

Random House and the colophon are registered trademarks of Random House LLC.

Visit us on the Web!
randomhouse.com/kids
Babymouse.com

Educators and librarians, for a variety of teaching tools, visit us at
RHTeachersLibrarians.com

Library of Congress Cataloging-in-Publication Data
Holm, Jennifer L.
Happy birthday, Babymouse / by Jennifer L. Holm & Matthew Holm. — 1st ed.
    p.   cm. — (Babymouse ; #18)
Summary: Babymouse imagines the biggest, most wonderful birthday party ever for herself and tries to make it happen, but Felicia is planning her own birthday bash for the very same day.
ISBN 978-0-307-93161-0 (trade pbk.) — ISBN 978-0-375-97097-9 (lib. bdg.) — ISBN 978-0-307-97544-7 (ebook)
[1. Graphic novels. [1. Graphic novels. 2. Imagination—Fiction. 3. Birthdays—Fiction. 4. Parties—Fiction. 5. Mice—Fiction.] I. Holm, Matthew. II. Title.
PZ7.7.H65Hap 2013 741.5'973—dc23 2012039798

MANUFACTURED IN MALAYSIA   10 9 8 7 6 5 4 3 2 1   First Edition

Random House Children's Books supports the First Amendment and celebrates the right to read.

TIMES SQUARE.

FIVE...FOUR...THREE...TWO...ONE...

YOU ARE INVITED TO: BABYMOUSE'S BIRTHDAY BASH!

WHERE: BABYMOUSE'S HOUSE

WHEN: 1:00 P.M. SATURDAY

I'VE ALWAYS WONDERED ABOUT SOMETHING, BABYMOUSE.

WHAT?

HOW OLD ARE YOU?

HUH?

YOU NEVER SAY IN THE BOOKS.

BOOKS? WHAT BOOKS?

MAINTAINING THE MYSTERY, I SEE.

17

SO WHO DID YOU INVITE, BABYMOUSE?

JUST A FEW PEOPLE.

TRIP!

GASP!

WHUMP!

27

SPLOOSH!

TAKE SOME MORE TEA.

WELL, IT IS SORT OF A ONE-MAN BAND AND ONE-MONKEY CIRCUS.

45

47

YOU DO KNOW WHAT HAPPENS TO THE GINGERBREAD MAN IN THE ORIGINAL FAIRY TALE, DON'T YOU?

WHAT?

I'LL TAKE THE ONE WITH THE MESSY WHISKERS.

THE NEXT DAY.

PETE'S REPTILE AND PIÑATA STORE

ZZZZZAAAPPP!

THE WORDS I WAS SEARCHING FOR WOULD BE "ABSOLUTELY ELECTRIFYING."

EEP.

GAME TIME.

OUCH!

POKE

PIN THE TAIL ON THE DONKEY!

CRUNCH!

JUMP!

JUMP!

OOF!

MUSICAL CHAIRS!

SPLASH!

BOBBING FOR APPLES!

SOB!

SWOOSH!

BABYMOUSE?

SIGH.

86

If you like Babymouse,
you'll love these other great books
by Jennifer L. Holm!

THE BOSTON JANE TRILOGY
EIGHTH GRADE IS MAKING ME SICK
MIDDLE SCHOOL IS WORSE THAN MEATLOAF
OUR ONLY MAY AMELIA
PENNY FROM HEAVEN
TURTLE IN PARADISE

AND DON'T MISS THE SQUISH GRAPHIC NOVELS BY MATTHEW HOLM AND JENNIFER L. HOLM:

#1   SQUISH: Super Amoeba

#2   SQUISH: Brave New Pond

#3   SQUISH: The Power of the Parasite

#4   SQUISH: Captain Disaster

#5   SQUISH: Game On!

And coming soon:

#6   SQUISH: Fear the Amoeba